D1379973

Emily Snape is a well-known children's author and illustrator whose work has appeared in books and magazines and on television around the world.

She lives in London with her three children and insists that none of them would ever attempt to turn each other into a guinea pig.

Fergus the Furball
by Emily Snape
Illustrated by Emily Snape

Published by Raven Books
An imprint of Ransom Publishing Ltd.
Unit 7, Brocklands Farm, West Meon, Hampshire GU32 1JN, UK
www.ransom.co.uk

ISBN 978 178591 850 6
First published in 2020

FERGUS THE FURBALL

Emily Snape

RAVEN

For Rufus, Iris and Clio x

 Chapter 1

OK, first of all, I need to get one thing completely straight.

THIS. WAS. NOT. MY. FAULT.

If I'd genuinely had any idea that my birthday wish was actually going to work, there are about a **million, gazillion** things I would have asked for, instead of this.

I've had nine attempts at birthday wish-making up to now, and not one of them has **ever** come true. Not even a tiny bit. And yes, you've guessed, that's one attempt for each birthday I've had.

I suppose the first few birthdays don't count. I was probably just thinking, "*Mmm* … CAKE!" or "*Oooo* … FIRE!" as everybody shouted, "Blow out the candles, Daniel, make a wish!"

Or I was busy filling my nappy. Mum says I used to do that a lot.

But, by the time I was seven years old, I'd really started putting a lot of thought into what to do with that special birthday wish.

For my seventh birthday, there was nothing I wanted more than a hoverboard. (OK, I know they don't exist. But that doesn't mean I couldn't wish for one.)

Anyway, as my robot-themed cake came near (it was awesome by the way, with red shoe-lace antennae and flying saucer eyes), I remember squeezing my eyes shut and blowing as hard as I possibly could.

I may have accidentally spat a bit on my

annoying little brother, Fergus. He was only five at the time, and started singing "Happy Birthday to you," like an opera singer. You know, with that <u>big voice</u> thing. So instead of looking at ME with loving expressions, my parents were busy fussing over Fergus. "Oh Fergus, you're a musical genius!"

Anyway, I just kept on pleading with the Universe for a sleek, green, floating board that I could rock up to school on every day, like a <u>super-hero</u>.

In the following weeks, I raced around our flat every morning to see if it had magically appeared. And every morning I was totally gutted when there was no sign of anything that could hover – even just a bit. I don't know how I thought it would happen, but I totally believed in the power of my birthday wish.

Well, of course, no hoverboard ever appeared. I didn't even get my hands on a skateboard that year, even though I begged my parents for one every single day. I ended up trying to make my own hoverboard with my mum's hair dryer and a tray. (I'll save you some time: it doesn't work – and my dad banned all my screen time for a week.)

On my **eighth** birthday I wished for a swimming pool. To be fair, I hadn't really thought this one through, considering we live in a third-floor flat which doesn't even have a bath. It would probably have needed to be a roof-top pool or something.

Anyway, two years later, we're still stuck with a **rubbish**, dripping shower that feels a bit like someone is weeing on your head. It's warm, too, so that's quite a realistic comparison, just in case you were thinking I was exaggerating.

My **ninth** birthday wish was a disaster and I'm so glad *that one* didn't come true. My parents

had let me take five friends to the trampoline park and, of course, "You have to invite your brother and sister to your party." (That was Mum speaking. And, yes, I'd also got an annoying little sister, Ruby, by then).

Well, we were all <u>exhausted</u> and sweaty after jumping non-stop for an hour (and Fergus had stolen all the attention as usual, with his stupid backwards somersaults). Anyway, when the gooey, marshmallow-decorated cake was shoved in front of me, I panicked. I couldn't remember what I'd been planning to wish for. My mind was <u>blank</u>.

My friends had finished singing "Happy birthday to you," and everybody was waiting, eyeing up the cake, when my wish idea shot back into my brain. I'd decided to ask for a private jet to Disneyland.

But then Fergus shouted, "Come on, POO FACE!" to me, so that was all I could think of.

Can you imagine how horrendous school would have been if that wish had come true and I'd ended up with poo for a face?

Like, forever?

Anyway, this year, you really can't blame me for what happened. It was half-past six in the morning, and I'd been dragged out of a lovely dream where a giant gummy bear was chasing my brother down the street.

 Chapter 2

The **problems** really began when my mum announced she had to go to Scotland for work. Of course, Dad thought it would be a 'good idea' if he went too, so my parents could spend some 'quality time' together.

It didn't sound like **my** kind of 'good idea'. It was pretty obvious to me that this wasn't just *not good* – it was a **terrible** idea!

"It's in two weeks' time,
Danny," Mum explained. (She always calls me
Danny when she's trying to butter me up. It
<u>never</u> works.)

"You mean the same two weeks' time as my
tenth birthday?" I replied.

I was stunned. Their trip was happening the
same week as my birthday! MY BIRTHDAY!
My <u>tenth</u> birthday, the one day where
everyone has to be super nice to me,

and make me breakfast in bed …

and fill the living room with balloons …

and …

and …

and …

I couldn't believe they were really going to do this to me.

"You don't mind, do you, Danny?" Mum pleaded. Of course I minded, but Mum insisted that it would be good for them.

For <u>THEM</u>!

Not for me, the birthday boy. Oh no, don't worry about me. I'm sure I'll have another tenth birthday at some point in my life! (That's sarcasm, by the way. Look it up.)

Then she told me that Aunt Tink (who's not even our real aunt), would come to look after us, and that they'd leave a really special gift for me to open on my big day.

As if that makes up for it.

Aunt Tink is my mum's oldest friend and, in a nutshell, she is completely mad.

↖ Aunt Tink & Mum

Like really <u>bonkers</u>.

She's into reading the future from bits of old tea – and she's always on about ghosts. Once she made me catch a ghost spider from her bathroom (I kid you not).

Woooo OOooo Do

17

And this is the responsible adult my parents had decided was suitable to leave us with.

ON MY BIRTHDAY!

Aunt Tink also looks off her rocker. She wears the weirdest clothes, like a huge, shaggy jacket in August and flip-flops with plastic daisies on them in December.

She's got huge, crazy orange glasses too.
(She says she's almost blind without them, but I
reckon the glasses shop saw her coming. I mean
it's not a choice of wearing huge, crazy orange
glasses or being blind, is it? She could wear
normal glasses, like most people. It's not *that*
hard to work it out.)

Every time she comes to visit us, her hair is
a different colour. (I like to make a bet with
Mum what she'll go for next, but neither of us
got it right last time, when she showed up with a
massive green afro).

She forgets everything, too, and is always

late, sometimes by days. She gets all sorts of things muddled up as well, like when Mum planned for us to all go to Legoland and she went to the Land of Leather instead. Or that time when we all went to an ice-cream parlour and she asked the waiter if she could have anything without ice or cream in it.

It can't be that hard being an adult.

"Mum, we won't survive if Aunt Tink is looking after us," I insisted.

"Well, Dad and I think it will be good for you to start looking after yourself a bit more. You know, get your own school clothes ready, like your younger brother already does ... "

[Ouch!]

" ... and make breakfast for your little sister. You're going to be ten soon."

Well, I'm glad she mentioned that. I mean, I'd **forgotten** already.

(More sarcasm.)

"It's only for a few days, Danny."

I scowled. The problem wasn't that it was just for a few days. The problem was, those few

days just happened to include the most
important day in the year!

I didn't really think my parents would
actually go on this Scotland trip. But they did,
just like that, at eight o'clock on Tuesday
morning. We were left with mad Aunt Tink for
<u>three</u> <u>whole</u> <u>nights</u> (and three whole days
as well, in case you hadn't worked that bit out).

It was obviously going to be a weird and a
not-how-I-had-planned-it tenth
birthday, but even *I* would
never have guessed how
crazy things were going to get.

Worst
Idea
EVER

Chapter 3

I tried to make myself feel better by rewriting all the rules for Aunt Tink, so I'd be able to do all the things Mum and Dad usually ban. Like **midnight** bedtimes and eating <u>seven bowls</u> of cereal for supper.

1. Watch TV till midnight.

2. Get an advance on my pocket money.

3. Eat 7 bowls of cereal for supper. Yum

I was up late into the night writing a long list of all these new rules, so I was **extra** bleary-eyed when Ruby (who's two and mostly cute – apart from when she's ganging up on me with Fergus), Fungus Brain himself and Aunt Tink all piled into my room at half-past six in the morning on April 7th.

(That was the day of my **birthday**, in case I hadn't made that clear. You know, my **tenth** birthday, the one where my parents decided to <u>abandon me</u>.)

Most days, I wake up with Fergus the Pergus

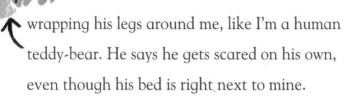

wrapping his legs around me, like I'm a human
teddy-bear. He says he gets scared on his own,
even though his bed is right next to mine.

I mean, seriously, can you imagine how
annoying it is to start your day with a sweaty,
pea-brained brother on top of you. Then,
when you moan about it, your mum says, "It's
just so sweet that he wants to cuddle up to you!"
Yeah, right.

Anyway, back to the very important
morning in question. In they all came, with Aunt
Tink carrying a huge, sticky chocolate cake.

I hate chocolate. I know you'll think I'm

weird, but I can't help it. It all started with a traumatic mix-up when I was three and I thought Fergus had **magically** created chocolate in his nappy. I think you can imagine the rest. Needless to say, he *hadn't* and it *wasn't*. (Sorry if I've just put you off chocolate for life.)

Right. So, back to the very important morning in question.

"Fergus made the cake all by himself!" Aunt Tink said proudly. "Isn't he the kindest? It looks delicious!"

Well, in Aunt Tink's world

"delicious" must mean "looks like poo".

I wouldn't have touched it even if the choice was between Fergus' cake and baked lizard tongue. That cake probably had Fungus Brain's snot mixed in with the icing.

I looked at the large, sticky brown mess in front of me. It had nine <u>wonky</u> candles (in four different colours) and I could see a <u>thumbprint</u> in the icing.

A cake with nine candles ... on my tenth birthday. That was all pretty annoying. The ridiculously early start didn't help either.

But it was the sound of Fergus singing

"Happy birthday to POOO!" that topped it off. Now I was sure. I was in a bad mood.

"Open presents, D-D!" Ruby beamed, waving her favourite toy rabbit in my face. Ruby takes Mr Bumbum everywhere (Fergus suggested that name of course, and it stuck) and she has him snugly tucked under one arm at all times (even on the swings, in the bath and when she's eating).

The first present Ruby handed me was a heavy box wrapped in icky, super-girly paper.

"That's from me, darling!" Aunt Tink announced. Of course it was.

I felt a bit nervous. Aunt Tink always gets us the strangest gifts. I shuddered just thinking about last year's present from her. She'd given me a small metal box with a jewel-encrusted monkey skull inside. I'm not joking. (Jewels I can understand, if they're worth loads of money, but what's with the monkey skull?)

So I peeled off this year's flowery paper a bit nervously. It was a dusty magic kit that looked about a million years old.

Printed on the faded cardboard box was a

picture of a
<u>really sinister</u>
magician with an evil
expression in his eyes.

I quickly shoved the box under my bed, in
case it had a dead rabbit or something equally as
horrendous inside.

"*Er* … thanks Aunt Tink," I mumbled.

"Do you like it?" she asked, hopefully.
"I remember how much you loved performing
shows for us when you were little!" Yeah, well,
that was before Fergus started stealing all the
limelight, I thought.

30

Ruby held out another present for me. "Is this from Mum and Dad?" I asked her. It was going to be a pet, I knew it. I'd been begging Mum and Dad for my own pet for as long as I could remember, and I was secretly super-excited.

But it had always been the usual excuses from my parents.

"We live in a flat, Daniel."

"We don't have anyone who can feed it when we go away, Daniel."

"Pet food costs money, Daniel."

Blah, blah, blah. Everyone I know has a pet. Even my best friend, Ethan, has a terrapin!

Ideally, I wanted a puppy, but I'd accept a kitten. Worst-case scenario, a fish would do. This year, I thought I'd finally cracked it with my constant whinging. (I knew it would work eventually.)

So I eyed the colourfully wrapped present Ruby was pushing towards me with excitement. There couldn't be a living creature in there, surely? It was <u>tall</u> and <u>lumpy</u> and actually quite <u>spikey.</u> A hedgehog maybe, if it was, say, standing up.

"Ow, stop it Ruby," I complained, as she shoved it into my arms.

"OPEN IT!" shouted Fergus in one of his super-irritating monster voices. He was deafeningly loud and shouted right into my ear, so I lost my hearing for about a minute.

I pushed him away and tried to prepare myself for disappointment. I'm ten now, I thought. I can handle this.

I tore off the paper.

Nothing in my ten years on this planet had prepared me for this.

Dear Daniel,
Sorry we couldn't get
you a dog, but here is
a lovely plant for you
to care for and nurture,
just like a pet.
Love M + D XXXX

My mum and dad had not got me
a pet. They had got me a
plant. An ugly, pointy,
misshapen cactus.

Fergus started to
snigger.

I was <u>FUMING</u>.

This was not how it was supposed to be on your
tenth birthday.

As Fergus' laughter pierced my brain, Aunt
Tink pushed the cake towards me, with its nine
wonky, lit candles. I had to back away so it
didn't singe my hair.

"Make your birthday wish, dearie!" she trilled. I glared at the lumpy cake and the horrible plant and my cackling brother. This was the <u>worst</u> <u>birthday ever!</u>

"Oh, I've just remembered I left the eggs boiling. Hold on!" Aunt Tink said, jumping up. Great! Hard-boiled eggs for breakfast too. Could it get any worse?

As Aunt Tink dashed out, an icy wind blew through the room, making the window frames rattle. It suddenly got really dark and the air felt all crackly – you know, like a storm was just about to begin.

I glared at Fergus. I'd wanted a pet, not a stupid plant, and I'd definitely never asked for a stupid brother.

"I wish … I wish I had a guinea pig instead of you," I hissed – and blew at the candles with a short, sharp puff. All nine candles went out instantly.

Chapter 4

At that moment, time seemed to go into slow

motion. A great roll of thunder and a flash of

white light filled the entire room, and

the ticking of the alarm clock

suddenly seemed eerily loud. Tick. Tock.

I rubbed my eyes. In the bright light of the

room, I could see Fergus still howling with

laughter. But it also looked like he was …
shrinking. Or was the room getting bigger?

Squinting, I peered at my
brother. His skin was changing
right before my eyes. It was
almost … *furry*. But the
worst thing was his face.

His big, blue eyes were morphing into small,
sinister black holes. His nose wrinkled up and
squished into a freakish triangular shape.

I shook my head in slow motion. Was
I dreaming? The cactus, still on my bed, jabbed
into my leg. I was still awake, then.

And now Fergus had disappeared. I stared at the Fergus-free space in front of me. Where on Earth was he?

"Fergie! Fergie!" Ruby cried, crouching down to where the wrapping paper lay on the floor. "Fergie furry!" she shouted.

A tufty little head peeped out near her foot. "A rat!" I screeched, jumping up. "Ruby, don't touch it. Dirty! Ruby! Dirty!"

"Fergie!" Ruby insisted, clapping her hands. "Fergie furry!" she chirped again. Then, to my horror, she put out her hand and let the fur ball climb onto it.

SPLAT!

"Drop it Ruby!" I screamed. I pushed her hand so the rat-thing fell onto the floor and scurried back under the paper.

"Fergie?" Ruby cried, welling up with tears. She bent down on all fours, looking under the bed. This is **ridiculous**, I thought, and sat down … directly on top of the chocolate cake.

"Ughhh!" I leapt up and twisted round to see lumps of mashed-up brown gooey-stuff smudged all over my pyjamas. A squeaky giggle came from somewhere down low. I spun round and looked straight into the eyes of the rodent, who was clearly smirking.

"Fergus!" I said, knowing at once that this strange, hairy creature was my brother.

Chapter 5

My heart began racing like mad. How was this possible? What would my parents say? I would SO be punished for this. What was the most likely penalty? Grounded for a week? No, worse than that. They'd get rid of the iPad. 100%. (Well Fergus wouldn't be able to use it any more, anyway.)

Mum and Dad could NOT find out that
I'd turned my brother into a … into a guinea
pig.

Was that really what I'd wished for? But
I didn't mean … My wishes never come true.
Why this one? Keep calm, I told
myself. There must be a logical
solution to this.

Ruby was sitting on the floor
stroking Fergus' little rodent
head and singing softly, "Baa baa,
Fergie … have you any wool?"

I whipped off my chocolate-covered pyjama

bottoms and then, remembering Aunt Tink, slammed the bedroom door.

"Fergus. Can. You. Hear. Me?" I said slowly and clearly, while pulling on yesterday's school trousers. Fergus nodded his tufty face, his floppy ears bouncing about.

A chill went down my spine. This was not good. This had to be worse than when I knocked out two of Fergus' teeth during a heated game of Monopoly. Even more terrible than when I opened Fergus' stocking up one Christmas, before he woke up …

In fact, this had to be near the top of the biggest *not good* list EVER.

"I'm going to sort this out. No one needs to know. Mum and Dad will NEVER find out. I'll just … *um* … unwish it!" I told my bedroom wall, trying not to be sick with the fear that had taken hold.

"I wish my brother was a human again," I told the wall, clearly and loudly. Then, after a pause, I added a gentle bleat: "*Please*."

Nothing happened.

"OK, right, no problem," I thought out loud. I just need to relight the candles and make the

wish as I blow them out again. That made sense.
I relit the candles with Aunt Tink's matches
(Mum would be horrified, but what else could
I do?) I took a deep breath and said, as clearly as
I could, "I wish my brother would turn back into
a human-being-boy, with no extra hair or whiskers
… right now. Pretty please. I'll never do
anything bad again … ever … I promise … "
And I blew out the candles.

I looked at Fergus, then at Ruby, and back
to Fergus. We all waited, in total silence, for
what seemed like forever. Come on Fergus!

I wished from the pit of my stomach to the

46

tips of my toes for Fergus to start growing back to his usual size again. But he just sat there, snuffling.

Suddenly Fergus squeezed his eyes shut and went a **worrying** shade of purple.

"Fergus!" I exclaimed, "What's happening?"

Fergus shuffled around, looking pleased with himself.

He picked up a small black pellet that had appeared on the floor. Was he ... ?

"Eeeew ... Fergus!" I screeched. "What are you doing?" My brother was actually eating his own rodent poo. Gross!

Normally my brother doing something so utterly disgusting would be <u>hilarious</u> (like when he accidentally swallowed his milk tooth and, as proof for the tooth fairy, searched his own **Number Twos** for a week). But nothing about this situation felt funny. Not one little bit.

"Please, stop doing that. Put your poo down and turn back into a human," I pleaded with him. "<u>Now!</u>"

"Daniel?" Aunt Tink's voice interrupted. Aunt Tink! I'd forgotten all about her.

"*Um* … I'm just getting dressed!" I yelled, trying to hide the panic in my voice.

"Fergus furry!" shouted Ruby, clambering to get out. I leapt in front of her and barricaded the door. I put on my best Strict Mum impression and whispered, "We are not going to tell Aunt Tink that Fergus is a guinea pig. ARE WE, Ruby?" My eyes pinned her to the spot.

"Aunty Tink!" Ruby shouted, beginning to cry.

"Shhh, Ruby." I tried to smother her in a bear hug. It seemed to shut her up briefly. I grabbed my T-shirt and used it to pick up my brother. "I can't believe I'm doing this," I whispered, as I put him carefully in my pocket.

OK, I thought. What next?

Chapter 6

"Your eggs are ready!" sang Aunt Tink as I stepped out into the hallway. The weight of the furry little body felt heavy inside my trouser pocket. My cheeks automatically flushed bright red.

"I'm afraid they are a little overdone. But I've mashed them and sprinkled some pepper on, so you shouldn't be able to tell, really."

Yu

"M*mmm*, thanks Aunt Tink," I stammered, heading to the kitchen. (I knew I had bigger problems, but really … <u>yuck!</u>) Ruby, my trusty sidekick, trotted speedily behind with Mr Bumbum wedged under her arm.

"Where's Fergus?" Aunt Tink asked. My face felt even hotter.

"Fergie furry!" Ruby explained. "Fergie guinea pig!"

I shot her a <u>deadly look</u>.

"Fergie furry!" the traitor said again.

"What's that, Rubes? Are you playing guinea pigs?" Aunt Tink got down onto the kitchen

floor on all fours and started snuffling around.
(I told you she was bonkers.)

Ruby wasn't impressed. She was staring at
me with her <u>BIG</u> eyes. Luckily, Aunt Tink
didn't seem to notice.

"So where *is* Fergus? Is he in the bathroom?"
Aunt Tink asked, looking around. "Your parents
said I had to keep a close eye on you two … "

"Fergus has actually, *er* … gone to school already," I stuttered.

"But it's only 7.30!" Aunt Tink said, puzzled.

"He has, *um* … violin practice," I garbled, as I spotted Fergus' violin case lying on the kitchen table.

"But he's forgotten his violin!"
Aunt Tink said, confused.

"That's all right, he'll just borrow one from the school," I heard myself explain. I was getting good at this. Lies were just rolling off my tongue.

By the way, can you imagine having a

brother that plays the violin? It's even **worse** than his singing or his __stupid__ impressions. And that's saying something. Mum and Dad even encourage him and say things like, <u>"How lovely!"</u> and "What beautiful playing!" And to me, "Why can't you learn an instrument, like Fergus?"

Are you **serious**? Why would I want to be like Fergus? He's a such a show-off. I've tried hiding his violin in the bin, under the car bonnet, in the fridge and once down the toilet (a bit obvious, I admit), but he just finds it and looks at me all hurt and innocent. He can't fool me – he's no angel. Just puts it on for Mum.

"Right, well, I'm off to have a shower, and then do I have to walk you to school or … ?" Aunt Tink looked panicked. Like she actually had to do something.

"No, no, it's fine, Aunt Tink. You just take Ruby to nursery," I bluffed.

"Great. Well, eat up your eggs and then you can have chocolate cake for dessert, birthday boy!" She crawled off, still on all fours.

I ignored the eggs and reached for Aunt Tink's phone, which she'd left lying on the kitchen table. There **must** be something on the internet that could get me out of this situation.

First I needed to get past the password. I tried tapping '1 2 3 4' on the screen and, just like that, I was in.

I shook my head in disbelief.

Adults really are dumb.

Chapter 7

I googled: What to do if you accidentally turn someone into a guinea pig.

A Guinea Pig Manual popped up.

I tried again. How to undo a birthday wish.
I flipped through the results, but they were all just junk.

"Come on then, Ruby, let's get you ready for

nursery!" Aunt Tink called, coming back into the kitchen with a towel wrapped around her hair. I quickly dropped the phone, hoping she wouldn't look at the screen. (Actually, I doubt if Aunt Tink has even heard of the internet).

I felt Fergus <u>squirm</u> in my pocket. I grabbed my coat and rushed to the front door. "I'm off now, see you later," I yelled, without looking back. I ran down the communal stairs and out onto the street.

"Fergus, you have got to stay still," I hissed at my trousers, glancing <u>suspiciously</u> around.

"I **will** sort this out. I'll find Ethan. He'll know what to do."

Ethan is my best friend and he knows about <u>all sorts</u> of stuff. He can make the fastest paper aeroplanes in the class. *And* he can cook lasagne from scratch.

Best meal EVER

Lasagne mmmmmm

I walked to school super-slowly. It was still really early and there was a weird, hazy morning glow after the thunderstorm. I watched the shopkeepers noisily opening their shutters, and smart people in suits sleepily sipping coffee as they headed to work. It was so strange to be

walking about with such a **massive** secret,
while everyone else carried on as normal.

"Hello, young Daniel," Mr Bertolini called
out from his restaurant (imaginatively called
Bertolini's) next to our block of flats. I tried not to
stare at his toupée, which sat **wonkily** on his
bald head. I looked around for his vicious dog,
but there was no sign of it. I've been going to
Bertolini's since I was a baby. They do the most
amazing pasta …

My stomach grumbled.

I hadn't eaten anything this morning.

"Morning Mr Bertolini," I replied, trying to

sound normal (and not like I'd turned my brother into a rodent).

"It's your birthday today, isn't it?" he smiled. "Here, let me get you a fresh croissant. My gift to you!" I took it thankfully and stuffed it into my mouth.

Fergus squeaked loudly in my pocket. I guess he was starving too, seeing as all he'd eaten so far this morning was a bit of his own poo. (I mean, no butter or sugar on it, not even a bit of milk to help it down. Yuck doesn't seem a strong enough word. But then I suppose it could have been worse. It could have been someone else's poo.)

I patted my pocket anxiously to shut him up.
Luckily Mr Bertolini was too busy writing out the
specials on his blackboard menu to notice. "I am
trying something new today," he explained.
"There's this Brazilian dish, *Cuy al palo*. It's a
craze on the internet."

"Yes … *mmm*, great,"
I mumbled, chomping through
the last of the croissant.

"I just need to get hold
of one tricky ingredient. Maybe you have an idea
of how to get it?" he said.

"Sure … *um* … of course."

"Roasted guinea pig!"

he smiled, gaps showing in his toothy grin.

"*Errr* ... " My stomach did a croissant-filled triple-somersault. "I've got to get to school," I yelped, and took off down the street.

"Keep up the good work," he called after me. "And keep an eye out for guinea pigs," he laughed.

I didn't turn around. I could feel Fergus jiggling about. Maybe he'd heard crazy Mr Bertolini. I put my hand on my pocket to keep him safe. I'd be in even **bigger** trouble if my brother got eaten before my parents got home from Scotland.

I arrived at school way too early, so I paced around the gates, waiting for Ethan to arrive. At last, I saw him whizzing up the road on his electric scooter. Why couldn't I have wished for one of those instead?

"Ethan! I've got something I need to tell you," I said to him urgently.

"Happy birthday, Dan," he beamed.

"Ethan, listen, this is really important."

"I don't have your present now. Mum said

I should bring it to your party on Saturday," he explained.

"Ethan, if you don't help me, there won't be a party on Saturday. Listen to me, please … "

"It's really cool, I know you're going to love it … " He was still rabbiting on.

"Ethan!" I shouted.

"Where's Fergus?" he asked, glancing around.

Ethan's an only child – lucky for him! He just doesn't get how annoying it is to have a little brother. Fergus is always hanging around, trailing behind us on the way home from school, crashing our gaming sessions and just trying to grab all the attention. I've told him over and over again to get lost, but he just doesn't listen. He's always there, trying to join in.

Ethan doesn't get it. He says I shouldn't be so mean to him and that Fergus is actually pretty funny (yeah, right). He has NO IDEA how unbelievably irritating Fergus really is.

"That's what I'm trying to tell you!" I hissed. I looked meaningfully at my pocket. But just then I felt a thump on my shoulder. It was Axel Buck, only the most evil boy

66

in school. He looks about eighteen, even though he's only just turned ten. And, yes, he's had it in for me since <u>FOREVER</u>.

"Birthday bumps for you today, Danny boy," he said, twisting my arm behind my back. "See you at break-time … or do I mean break-a-leg time, mate?"

My palms suddenly felt sweaty and a dull ache started in the pit of my stomach.

Chapter 8

"Quieten down, everybody," Mrs Moosh, our teacher, said in her soft, sing-song voice. As usual, everyone ignored her.

She is **mega-drippy**. She's into all that hippie stuff like yoga and she only wears clothes that are grey or beige.

She's got huge round glasses too, that make

her look like a snowy owl. I've never heard her raise her voice.

"Hush, hush," she repeated warmly, dinging a little triangle she keeps on her desk (like that makes a difference – she'd need a foghorn to shut us lot up).

"Today, we are going to talk about *Wellness*," I heard over the din. There was a massive groan. Her lips were moving, but I couldn't concentrate on what she was saying. All I could think about was my brother shrinking right before my eyes and

his face turning all rodenty. Could that really have happened this morning? This was the worst birthday <u>EVER</u>.

I was suddenly aware of a warm feeling spreading over my leg. I glanced down and realised my trousers were soaked.

I stared in disbelief. My trousers had quite clearly changed from light to dark grey. Had Fergus just peed in my pocket?

I jabbed at the Fergus lump angrily. "<u>What have you done?</u>" He squeaked audibly, so I jabbed at him again.

"Is everything alright, Daniel?" Mrs Moosh

looked across at me and the class fell silent.

"*Mmmm ...* " I managed to say, as Fergus squeaked even more loudly.

"You're ... *squeaking*, Daniel," Mrs Moosh said in a puzzled voice. I sank as low as I could into my chair. I could feel the whole class staring at me. I flashed Ethan a hopeless look, but he shrugged, obviously baffled.

On the board Mrs Moosh had written:

Personal Mantra
Find your own special word
to meditate to

71

"My mantra, Miss," I mumbled and, on cue, Fergus made his <u>loudest</u> squeal.

"Perfect, just what I needed. A volunteer." Mrs Moosh smiled sweetly. I looked at her in horror. No, *please*, no … Let me just sit here and pretend my life hasn't gone into a free-fall disaster.

"Pop up to the front, Daniel. You can demonstrate to everyone how you practice your mantra. How interesting that you chose a squeak as your personal relaxation sound. Why don't you tell us how you came up with that?"

I sat frozen, as still as a statue. Maybe if I just

stayed here, not moving, everyone might forget I exist. Or the world might explode – and take the damp patch on my trousers with it.

"Daniel?" Mrs Moosh prompted.

OK, the statue idea clearly wasn't going to work. I looked at the door to the classroom and I looked down at my soaking trousers. Then I grabbed my workbook, held it in front of the wet patch and raced out of the classroom.

I sprinted down the hallway towards the boys' loos, shouting behind me, "Had chocolate cake for breakfast, going to be sick! Sorry!"

Chapter 9

Slamming the cubicle door, I tried to catch my breath. Fergus was **wriggling** in my wet pocket, so I pulled him out and we sat there, staring at each other (both trying to ignore the **disgusting** toilet smell).

"You peed on me!" I whispered, outraged. He squeaked.

"You weed on my actual leg, dude!"

He squeaked again.

This was worse than when he wouldn't stop talking. How could I have a fight with a rodent that only knew one word ("Squeak")?

"I hate you. You're always ruining my life!"

Even as a guinea pig, Fergus still managed to do the puppy-dog-eye thing and look all sad, which makes everyone (apart from me) feel sorry for him.

Usually, at this point in an argument with Fergus, I'd throw the TV remote

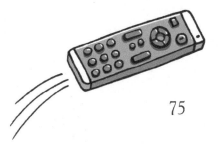

at him, or say something that made him go
running to Mum, so I would get sent to my room.

But what was I supposed to do now?

I shoved him back into my pocket and
opened the cubicle door. Thankfully, the toilets
seemed empty. I glanced around to double-check,
then started up the hand dryer.

I had to stand on one leg and sort of hug the
wall, so the hot air would dry my trousers as
quickly as possible.

After spending ages with my finger on the
'on' button to keep it going, I realised Fergus'
squeaks were even higher pitched than before.

And he was <u>thrashing around</u> rather a lot.

"Oh man!" I yelled. I never meant to slowly roast my brother with hot air. I yanked him out of my trousers and threw him into the sink, before running the cold tap over his hot, furry little body.

He looked up at me, his black beady eyes welling with tears, as the sink filled up like a tiny swimming pool. All he needed was a rubber ring.

"Well, this is all your fault," I said bitterly. "If you hadn't been so annoying

I wouldn't have made that <u>stupid</u> wish ... "

I trailed off, feeling a little bit guilty. His whiskers did look a bit singed and his fur ... well, let's just say it didn't look good.

I picked him up and we stared at each other, eye to eye. I was thinking maybe I should kind-of apologise. I don't mean actually saying the 'S' word – I make sure <u>I never</u>, <u>ever</u>, say that to Fergus-face. (Unless I'm muttering, "Sorry you were ever born.")

But maybe I owed him a: "*I guess I shouldn't have wished for you to become a cuter version of a rat.*" But then he violently shook off the water, like a mad dog jumping out of a stream, sprinkling it all over my face.

Nope. I didn't owe him anything.

"Fergus!" I cried, snapping my head back. His grimy rodent water had gone right up my nose. The sound of a door opening made us both jump, and I quickly crammed him into my now-dry pocket.

Ethan charged into the room. "Dan, are you OK?"

"No!" I shouted. Finally I could tell Ethan about the mess I was in.

"Were you sick? Eeeww, lemmee see!" he grinned.

"No, yuck. You're not going to believe it,
but … " I stuttered, trying to work out how to
actually *say it*. Keep to the facts, I told myself.
I took a deep breath. Just come out with it …
"I wished Fergus was a guinea pig and then he
turned into one. Right in front of me and Ruby. And,
well, I've got him here in my pocket, right now."

I paused to let it sink in. "Seriously, mate,
I don't know what to do. Mum and Dad are
going to kill me if they find out."

Ethan stared at me <u>dumbstruck</u>. Then he
started to laugh. Great big belly laughs. "You
crack me up, Dan," he grinned. "You look so

serious. Unbelievable," he said, strolling
out of the toilets, still chuckling.

"Ethan!" I shouted after him, following
him back into the hallway.

"I've got drum practice now," he called. "See
you after break." He disappeared into the crowds
of pupils pushing to get into the playground.

I got shoved along with everyone else until
I found myself out in the fresh air. I pulled my
jumper down hard over my pockets and paced up
and down, trying to work out what to do.

Well, at least there's no way things can
possibly get any worse, I thought.

Chapter 10

"We need you in goal, Dan!" My mate Omar grabbed me by the shoulders. I was about to say "No," but I could see Axel Buck coming towards me. "Come on, Dan," Omar urged. I didn't need telling twice. I quickly legged it to the safety of the football cage and positioned myself between the goalposts.

Fergus was jiggling about in my pocket as
I hopped from foot to foot, keeping an eye out for
the ball. "Stay still!" I hissed. At least football
was the one thing I had over on Fergus. He
couldn't kick a ball to save his life. But me? *I* was
like a machine on the pitch.

The ball sped towards me and, before I knew
it, I was on auto-pilot, diving in a perfect arch ...

"GOOOALLLLL!" I heard a voice
call, as the ball flew past me and into the net.
I landed on the concrete
ground with a
heavy thud.

My first thought was: I can't believe I missed that goal. My second thought was: I've just squashed Fergus!

I jumped up and jiggled my trouser leg a bit, but there was no movement. Nothing. He was totally still. I could tell he was still tucked deep in my pocket, but he just … wasn't moving.

I turned to face the goal and bent down towards my pocket. "Fergus … " I whispered. "Are you dead?"

Still nothing. This wasn't good. I pulled his floppy little body out of my pocket and gently stroked his furry tummy.

"Are you OK?" I asked pleadingly. "Fergus, squeak … please?"

"Dan! You've just let in another goal," Omar shouted, as the ball sailed past me again. "What are you doing? Is that … hey, **what** is that?" he asked, intrigued.

"What's birthday boy got, then?" Axel's gruff voice echoed. I held Fergus close.

"Did you get a cuddly-wuddly toy for your birthday?" Axel mocked in delight. I felt my cheeks flush and heard a bubble of laughter from the other kids.

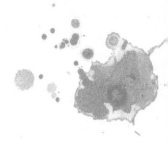

"It is <u>not</u> a cuddly toy … " I stammered.

"Ahhh, how sweet. Give it here … " he said, snatching at Fergus.

"No!" I shouted. I swung away from Axel's beefy grasp and Fergus shot right out of my hand … THUNK! … and lay completely still on the cold, hard floor.

Axel made a swipe for Fergus but, to my utter relief, Fergus limped back towards me and I picked him up.

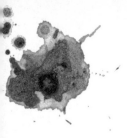

"You're alive!" I whispered to him, grinning from ear to ear.

"Woah! Is that a robot guinea pig?" Omar asked.

"Er... yeah," I bluffed.

"What can it do, then?"

"*Um*, it's voice-activated, it can ... *er*, do anything, I think!" I said.

My knees were still shaking a bit. I was feeling grateful that I hadn't just <u>flattened</u> my brother into a pancake.

"Show us, then," Omar urged.

"<u>OK, well, walk forward</u>," I commanded.

I was seriously hoping Fergus would play along and get us out of this mess.

He hesitated for a moment, then he marched forward obediently.

"Now backwards … "
I tried, and Fergus trotted backwards on his little legs. "Roll over … jump up … now do a forward roll."

Fergus was <u>brilliant</u>! There was a crowd of kids around us now, all shouting instructions at Fergus.

"I want one. It's awesome!' said Omar.

"Yeah, me too. Where did you get it?" someone else asked.

"Can it do a back-flip?" Nicola, from the year above, asked. Sure enough, Fergus performed a perfect back-flip. (He's always been really good at acrobatics, and I get dragged along to all his stupid competitions.)

"It's the <u>Guinea Pig 9000</u>," I glowed, enjoying myself now. "I got it this morning, from my Aunt Tink for my birthday." I thought about the rotten gift she'd actually got me. That old magic set, with the sinister magician's face on the cover. I shuddered.

"Right, break-time's over," a teacher's voice called out. I stuffed Fergus back in my pocket.

"You smashed it!" I whispered, and I meant it. He was amazing.

"You're so lucky," Omar said, as he walked past. I felt a wash of pride come over me as I headed back to class.

Chapter 11

Back in class, Mrs Moosh had already begun our new topic on animal senses. "We are beginning with mammals," she said, "and we are lucky enough to borrow Class 4B's pet, Otis, this afternoon."

I couldn't concentrate on anything she said. I needed to focus on the <u>real</u> <u>problem</u>, which was getting Ethan to believe that I had accidentally transformed my brother into a small rodent. And then we had to figure out how to switch him back into a human.

Easy-peasy. NOT!

Ethan was two desks away from me.

I glanced over. Once Ethan realises I'm telling the truth, he'll know what to do, I thought. He always does.

Like when he got my bike out of the canal using an old broom handle. Or when he helped me move the coffee table, so my parents never found out about that huge hole we made in the living room wall. OK, maybe this was a bit different, but he was bound to come up with a solution.

I scribbled a note:

I was being SERIOUS before.
I MEANT what I said.

I folded it in half and wrote E on the front, then passed it to Omar. He glanced at it and tossed it towards Ethan. But instead, it bonked Eugenie Middleton on the nose and landed in her sparkly pencil case.

"<u>Nooooooooooooooo!</u>" I screeched in

my head. She was <u>bound</u> to tell the teacher.
I was on my very last warning at school, and if
Mrs Moosh caught me swapping notes I was
going to have to miss lunch break. And then
what? I'd **never** fix my brother at this rate.

Eugenie Middleton had transferred to our
school last term, from some super-posh school
somewhere or other. She's a super-posh school
sort of person, down to her <u>unbelievably</u> shiny
shoes and ironed socks.

(Who on Earth irons their socks? I think
anybody who irons their socks has got some real
issues. That's all I'm saying. I can't even manage

to find a pair of matching socks, and all my
school socks are black).

She's the first one to shoot her hand up
whenever Mrs Moosh asks a question, as well,
and she <u>always</u> knows the correct answer to
everything.

You know the sort.

Anyway, I rolled my eyes and waited for her
to tell Mrs Moosh I'd been passing notes, but she
didn't. Instead she opened it, read it, and then,
to my amazement, started writing her own note.

When Omar passed it back to me I could see
he was stifling giggles. I scowled at him. I did

not want anyone to think I was passing <u>ANY</u>

sort of notes with Eugenie Middleton.

She'd written back, in perfect, loopy writing.

Serious about what?

Meet you behind

the bikesheds

at lunch.

E

She stared straight ahead at the teacher.

"Oh great," I sighed, scrunching it up.

"Daniel!" Mrs Moosh sounded surprised.

"I hope you have been paying attention and not

day-dreaming again. Remember, you are on your final warning."

I flushed and looked as if I was paying attention.

"Now, tell me what the answer is then, please?" she asked. The room was silent.

"Could you repeat the question, Miss?" I asked slowly.

Mrs Moosh sighed. "Guinea pigs ... "

I sat up straight.

"Do they possess the ability to hear a) ultra-high frequency sounds, or b) extremely low sounds?"

I gulped.

"Daniel?" Mrs Heath prompted. "Is the answer **a)** … " Fergus made a little kick at my thigh from inside my pocket. " … or **b)**?"

"It's **a)**, Miss," I said, hoping Fergus wasn't landing me in trouble.

"Correct, excellent," she replied and carried on talking.

My shoulders relaxed. "Thanks, bro," I whispered.

At last, the lunch bell rang. I grabbed Ethan. I was desperate to get him on his own so I could pick his brains (not literally, that would be gross).

98

"Omar told me about your robot! Can I see?" Ethan grinned.

"It's <u>not a robot</u>," I hissed, dragging him towards the lunch hall.

"Oh yeah, it's really Fergus, isn't it?" Ethan laughed, shaking his head.

How was I going get him to believe me? We got in the queue for food and the dinner lady dumped grey mashed potato and a rock-hard sausage on my plate. Moving along, I was handed a wobbly red jelly.

Red jelly. I felt bad. Red jelly was Fergus' absolute favourite. He was probably starving.

What did guinea pigs eat anyway
(apart from their own poo?)

Ethan and I sat down in our usual spot.
I took a pinch of jelly and sneaked it into my
pocket. Fergus licked away at my fingers
greedily. His little tongue was rough and wet.

"Gross ... " I shuddered.

"Don't you like the mash? I'll have it," Ethan
smiled greedily.

"Feel free. I've totally lost my appetite,"
I explained. Having my little brother lick my
fingers is not my idea of a good time. But I
suppose he is my brother and he did, surprisingly,

give me the right answer in class. I carefully
shoved a little more jelly into my pocket.

"Ow!" I howled. "You bit me!" Fergus had
nipped my little finger!

I jumped up and hurled Fergus out of my
pocket. He stayed motionless on the ground for a
second. Then he looked up at me. He seemed to
be squeaking, "Sorry."

Suddenly I was aware of Axel's hefty bulk
towering next to us.

"Give us a go on your Guinea Pig 9000," he
growled. I panicked and looked down, but Fergus
was gone.

101

Chapter 12

I looked around anxiously, but Fergus was **nowhere** to be seen. He must have scuttled into hiding. Meanwhile, Axel was peering under tables and kicking people's legs.

"Tell your robot to come here!" Axel barked.

I shook my head.

"Give it to me, or when I find it I'm going to

smash it up and feed it to my toaster." His giant hand tightened into a gnarly fist.

"You're never going to get it, so just give up looking," I spluttered.

Axel raised his left foot up high, looked at me right in the eyes and stamped down hard on my toes.

"Owwwwwwwwwww!!"

"What's going on here?"

Typical. Mrs Moosh had turned up right after the damage had been done, as always. My foot was throbbing like mad.

"I was just wishing Danny-boy a happy

birthday, Miss," Axel said in a mock-charming voice.

"That's lovely, Axel," Mrs Moosh smiled. "Now run along into the playground, boys. It's the lower years' turn in the lunch hall." And she shooed us out into the sunlight.

"Are you all right?" Ethan said, shaking his head. I shrugged. My foot was still pounding, 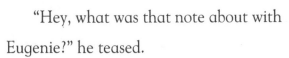 but I had bigger problems.

"Hey, what was that note about with Eugenie?" he teased.

"It was for you, dummy!" I exclaimed.

"Well, I think *she* wants to talk to *you*!" He

pointed to the bike shed, where Eugenie was waving enthusiastically at me.

I sighed.

Better get this over and done with, I thought, as I marched over to her. Ethan scuttled along behind me.

"Hey, Daniel. Happy birthday!" she smiled, with her **perfect** dimples.

I stared at her. Why wouldn't this girl just shove off?

"So what were you trying to tell me in class?" She looked up at me expectantly.

"I wasn't trying to tell YOU anything," I replied.

"What is the matter, Dan?" Ethan asked. "You've been totally stressed all day! All that stuff about your brother turning into a guinea pig ... " he laughed. "You're a few sprinkles short of a sundae!"

I felt totally defeated. Now I didn't even have Fergus to prove it.

Ethan was enjoying himself. "You're a few Smarties short of a tube ...

… a few bananas short of a bunch …

… a few fries short of a Happy Meal … "

"Hang on," Eugenie interrupted. "Your brother is a … a *guinea pig*? I've heard of some dysfunctional families, but that's a new one!"

Dysfunctional? Who in the world – except Eugenie Middleton – is going to use a word like that in a normal sentence?

I ignored her. "No one is ever going to believe me," I told Ethan pathetically. "This might seem like a joke to you, but I have done

the worst thing EVER and I have no idea how to undo it. And Fergus is probably going to end up flattened under somebody's shoe!"

"Take it easy, Dan," Ethan said, looking a bit embarrassed for me. "*Er ...* Maybe you should just go, Eugenie," he said, glancing at her. Ethan obviously thought I was losing it.

"Well, I think you're telling the truth," she said softly.

I looked up, confused. "Are you kidding?" I asked slowly. I'd never noticed before that Eugenie had a sense of humour.

"There's this book I've been reading in the library," she explained. (Uh oh! That figures. Other kids get excited about football, or YouTube.) "It's about **metamorphosis** in magic. It's really fascinating." She actually looked like she meant it.

"You … you **believe** me?" I stuttered.

"It's called **shapeshifting**. Apparently it's been reported in almost all cultures throughout history."

I looked at her blankly.

"Tell us exactly what happened, Daniel."

So I did.

Chapter 13

I told them **everything** that had happened that morning, even down to the chocolate-smudged pyjamas and Mr Bertolini's hunt for skinned guinea-pig meat.

Ethan looked pretty confused, but Eugenie was busily writing all the facts down in a little notebook.

" … and now I've lost him," I finished, a lump in my throat. "If Axel finds him before me, he's … I don't even want to **imagine** what he's going to do. Turn him into grated guinea pig most probably." I gulped.

"Axel is a **creep**," Eugenie exclaimed. "He squished my satsuma yesterday with his bare hands – right in front of me. Then he licked the juice off his own arm. It was disgusting."

Ethan and I winced. *Yuck.*

I didn't realise Axel picked on Eugenie too. I guess I'd never really taken much notice of her – except for thinking she was a goody-two-shoes.

111

I'm not sure if we'd ever spoken more than one word to each other before. I looked at her properly for the first time and noticed she had a Black Wasp badge.
(Black Wasp are literally the best band ever
– check them out.)

Could it be … was Eugenie Middleton actually *alright*?

"I was so chuffed" (she honestly used the word chuffed) "you passed me that note today," Eugenie blushed. "I really miss my friends from my old school."

I tried not to roll my eyes as she mentioned her <u>perfect</u> old school again. This wasn't the right time.

"So anyway, thanks," she said, her face lighting up.

I stared down hard at my dangling shoelaces. I wasn't used to this sort of chat.

"You should tie those up," Eugenie exclaimed. That sounded more like the Eugenie I was used too. I felt relieved.

"Right. Back to the current problem. Step one, we find Fergus," she said, with such a

commanding voice I felt
myself stand up a bit taller.

Ethan still didn't look
convinced. "I'll help you find 'Fergus' … " (He
actually said "Fergus" with finger quote marks.
He still didn't believe me!) " … but we need a
mission code name. How about … FURBALL!"
Ethan looked delighted with himself. I rolled my
eyes. This was serious!

"We should split up," Eugenie said, taking
command. "Ethan, you check the … "

"My spy name is Laser Shark," Ethan
interrupted her, with a smug grin.

"OK, fine, Laser Shark, you check the playgrounds, the football cage and the water fountains," she commanded. "Daniel, you search the lunch hall, the stairs and the toilets. I will inspect the classrooms, the school office and staff room. And Mrs McDoom's office. We meet back here in ten minutes sharp!"

I looked at her warily. Mrs McDoom is our terrifying head teacher (we all call her Dr Doom behind her back). If Dr Doom was an animal, she would be a

spider. She's small **and** terrifying. She sweeps
silently around the school and spits spider venom
if she spots you trading football cards with your
friends.

"How are you going to get away with
sneaking around the teachers in the staff room?"
I asked Eugenie. "And you're <u>never</u> going to
get to snoop around **all** the classes, especially
Dr Doom's lair, without getting in trouble."

Eugenie rolled her big, brown eyes.
"I am the **brightest,
best-behaved** girl in the
school, dumbo! No one **ever**

suspects me of doing anything wrong!" She grinned. "I just say whatever I want with utter conviction and everyone believes me." She smiled. "You should try it!"

"OK, OK," I replied weakly. How I'd complicated my problems by adding Eugenie Middleton into the mix was beyond me, but at least she was willing to help. And she seemed to have her head screwed on right.

She gave us the nod and we all headed off in our assigned directions. Ethan pinned himself to

the wall in full undercover agent mode. "The Fergus hunt, I mean <u>MISSION FURBALL</u>, begins!" he whispered.

"It's going to be fine," I told myself, trying out Eugenie's suggestion. Say things with conviction and everyone will believe you. Could I make it work on myself? I really missed the feeling of Fergus' miniature body in my pocket. "This is all under control," I said positively. "One of us will find him, and then we'll get him back into human form, for sure."

I started by looking in the boys' toilets. "Fergus, are you in here?" I whispered into the empty room. Nothing.

"All right?" Omar said, startling me as he barged out of a cubicle.

"Yep, good, fine," I muttered, and swiftly exited the loos.

I stared at the door of the girls' toilets next. Did I <u>really</u> have to check in there?

I took a deep breath, pushed the door open and poked my head in. Five girls screamed at me and slammed the door in my face.

"Did you just go in the girls' loos?" Omar asked <u>suspiciously</u>, as he swung out of the boy's toilets.

"No," I said, with conviction, applying Eugenie's advice.

"Whatever," he said and jogged off.

It worked! He believed me! Eugenie was right. Wow! "Where was I meant to look next?" I wondered. "The stairs next, wasn't it?" I marched towards them.

I looked around for anything small and furry.

"Got your robot back?" Axel shattered my concentration as we crossed on the stairs.

The hairs on the back of my neck prickled. At least he hadn't got hold of Fergus – yet.

"Axel Buck and Daniel Rogers." Dr Doom's icy voice shot in our direction. She appeared, spider-like, at the top of the stairs. "You should both be in your classroom. Lunch break is over."

Chapter 14

Ethan and Eugenie were already sitting at their desks. They both shook their heads at me.

"<u>Where was Fergus?</u>" a voice screamed inside my head.

"Class," Mrs Moosh addressed us, "as you know, we are all really excited to have Otis in our classroom today … "

Who was Otis again? A foreign exchange student? A teaching assistant?

But she was pointing at the hutch on her desk. I looked at it properly now. I could make out a small, hairy ball. Was it … ? Yes … there was a guinea pig in the hutch. No! There were TWO guinea pigs in there. One in a terrified, rolled-up position, and the other staring out indignantly at us, with its nose squished up to the prison walls of the metal bars.

My heart started thumping in my chest.

" … but there appears to have been some sort of practical joke. Mrs McDoom found Otis running around the school lunch hall today after everyone had finished their food. But when she brought him back to his cage, 'Otis' was already in there."

Everyone stared blankly at Mrs Moosh.

"There seem to be two Otises," she clarified. "Can anyone here please explain how we have suddenly doubled our guinea pig population? Does anyone know where this extra creature comes from, or to whom it belongs?"

I looked at Otis One and Otis Two. One of these animals had to be my brother. They looked identical.

A hand shot up. "Yes, Cleo? Can you shed light on this situation?"

"Otis must have had a baby!" Cleo exclaimed brightly.

"No, Cleo." Mrs Moosh looked at the ceiling and sighed. Another arm at the back of the class was waving frantically.

"Omar?"

"It could be Daniel's robot toy, the Guinea Pig 9000!"

I swallowed.

"I can assure you, Omar, this guinea pig is real. It did an … ahem … a *faeces* in Mrs McDoom's hands when she carried it back here."

"Go, Otis!" Omar guffawed, and the class broke out into fits of giggles.

Oh Fergus, I smiled to myself, you genius!

I looked at Ethan. He was as white as a sheet and seemed in shock. Had he at last begun to believe me now? I longed to whisper "Fergus?" at the hutch, to see which one was my brother. Luckily I stopped myself, before everyone thought I was a **complete loony**.

Both of the guinea pigs had little pink noses. They both had dark, beady eyes and short brown fur. The angry-looking one at the front of the cage was quite a bit bigger than the other. Could that be Fergus?

Fergus was actually quite short for his age and was still wearing last year's school uniform (something I often liked to remind him about). Maybe I shouldn't make so much fun of him. Maybe he'll **never** be able to wear a school uniform again. Could he borrow Ruby's doll's

clothes? No, I told myself, shaking my head. I had to sort this out.

If I was trapped in a hutch with a **massive** hairy creature who had <u>sharp</u> fang-like teeth and ominous black eyes, I think I'd be the one at the back hiding, pretending to be a piece of the furniture.

So, to be honest, Fergus could be either of them.

"Right, well, if no one can give us any clarity on this very strange problem, we will have to carry on our lesson, and hope to resolve it before the end of the day."

Mrs Moosh didn't sound very confident. Wow, poor Fergus. What had I done? This was a disaster. I couldn't concentrate on Mrs Moosh. I just kept looking at the two guinea pigs, trying to spot that scar I'd accidentally given Fergus the time we turned our house into a ghost train.

That had been a good day. We'd had all our cousins over and charged them 20p each for a once-in-a-lifetime spooktacular adventure. Mum wasn't that impressed when she saw we'd transformed the shower into a shaving foam and bubble bath pit. Or when she realised we'd

locked our cousin Tabby in the <u>Wardrobe of Death</u> (and lost the key). She went ballistic when she saw the Swamp of Doom Fergus had created in the communal garden. But we'd made 60p and it had been loads of fun. I'd dressed Fergus up as a one-eyed monster with spaghetti brains pouring out of his skull. It had all got quite slippery. That's sort of how the scar bit happened.

As I thought more about it, I realised there had actually been quite a lot of good days with Fergus. I remembered our epic den-making.

Once we'd slept out in one all night and I'd dared Fergus to eat his own toenail. Then, to make up for it, I'd made a midnight feast with microwaved crackers and melted cheese that we called Space Invader Biscuits.

I didn't want my brother to stay 15cm tall. I loved him. A tear trickled down my cheek. I want my brother back! This isn't fair! **I never** meant the wish to come true.

"Miss, Miss!" Omar suddenly shouted with glee, making me jump guiltily. "Otis One is spraying wee all over Otis Two!"

We all stared at the hutch.

It was true. Otis Two was backing even further into the corner of the hutch, pressing its little body against the back wall, whilst the bulky one was shooting yellow wee all over it.

Ughhh!

"Oh, goodness!" Mrs Moosh flushed.

"I know what's happening,"

Eugenie's hand shot up. She flashed me a sympathetic glance.

"Yes, Eugenie?"

"Female guinea pigs can squirt jets of urine at males … when they want them to go away!"

"One of the Otises must be a girl then!" Ethan added, gleefully.

<u>Poor Fergus</u>. Well, now at least we knew which one he was! The one soaked in warm guinea-pig wee.

Chapter 15

Ding! The home-time bell rang and everyone began to spill out of class. Time for **Mission Furball!** Ethan and Eugenie started to distract Mrs Moosh with questions. I had to grab my brother. This was my moment. I couldn't waste a second.

"That was a **really great** lesson, Miss,"

Ethan was saying, pulling Mrs Moosh towards the door and winking at me. "Will Otis be in our class tomorrow? What do guinea pigs eat, Miss?"

"Why are guinea pigs called guinea pigs, Mrs Moosh?" Eugenie inquired.

'Um … " Mrs Moosh seemed a little dazzled by all the sudden attention.

"How long do they live for?" I heard Ethan ask. My ears pricked up. I was worried what the answer might be. I looked over, but Ethan gave me a 'get on with it' sort of look.

So I leapt to the hutch, unhooked the little door and dipped my hand in, grabbing an

135

unpleasantly moist Fergus. Otis One ran at me, biting into my hand. I made a silent yelp while whisking my brother to the safety of my pocket.

Mrs Moosh spun around, but Eugenie brilliantly dropped her pencil case and books all over the floor. She apologised, grabbed her stuff, and then we all legged it out of there and ran to the school gates as fast as we could.

We were out! We rushed down the street, away from school, and I held on to my pocket firmly so there was no chance of Fergus falling out.

"We did it!" I laughed, "I've got him, I've got my brother back! <u>Everything's OK</u>!"

"He's still a guinea pig." Ethan responded flatly, as we slowed down. I fell back down to Earth.

"So you believe me now?" I asked.

"I guess so," he replied. "But it's pretty hard to take in. And even assuming Fergus really *is* a guinea pig and you haven't completely lost your mind, what are you going to do?" he asked. "I think you need to tell your parents."

"What! Are you kidding? They will <u>kill</u> me. That's the stupidest idea I've ever heard."

"This is **serious**, Dan. If it's really true, you **have** to tell them what's happened."

"Tell my parents? You're crazy. They must <u>NEVER</u> know! They'd disown me! I thought you'd know how to fix this!" I cried.

"Well, I have an idea," Eugenie was saying, but we both ignored her.

I was shouting at Ethan quite loudly now. "You're supposed to be MY **best friend!**" I screamed, "not on Fergus' side!"

"It's not **my fault** you got yourself into this mess! You could've wished for **anything**! We could be flying home right now on a magic

138

carpet. Or going back to your private island, made of chocolate … "

"I <u>hate</u> chocolate," I spat.

"Well, I don't know why you're angry at me. *I* didn't do it." Ethan grunted and started to walk off in a huff.

"I have an idea," Eugenie bellowed, making me jump, "when you've finished your stupid squabble." Ethan looked back at both of us. I opened my mouth to keep arguing, but then wisely closed it again.

"What's your idea, then?" Ethan asked quietly.

Chapter 16

"So there's this book … " Eugenie explained. "You can't take it out of the library."

"I thought that was the idea of libraries," I muttered. She ignored me.

"You can only look at it in this <u>special room,</u> with its own temperature to protect the books. There's a collection of really rare maps

and there's a recipe book from the Middle Ages, too … "

"And how would that help us?" I asked, frustrated. "No one is cooking my brother."

"No, not that one. There's this other book, *A History of Metamorphosis*. It's beautiful."

"Sounds it!" I spluttered sarcastically.

"It is," Eugenie responded coolly. "It's about a hundred years old and it's full of detailed illustrations. It even has legends from Atlantis! There's a lot of fables and folklore about people transforming into animals. It might have something in it that could help."

"A <u>book</u>," I replied, dumbfounded. "My brother is in my pocket and now has four feet. And we're going to look at a book?"

"Well, it's somewhere to start," she suggested, shrugging. She paused, looking at me. "Or shall we all just go home?"

Ethan and I kept our mouths shut and followed her to the library.

When we got to the library entrance, Eugenie stopped. "Don't take this personally," she began. I was pretty sure that, whatever she said next, I *would* be taking it personally.

"I'm not sure if Mr Kank will let you two into the Archive Room."

"The what?" we asked in unison.

Eugenie rolled her eyes. "You have to apply for **permission**, and they don't grant it to just <u>anybody</u>." (Sure! Not offensive at all, I thought.)

Eugenie carried on without batting an eyelid. "I have a membership card from my old school. I think I could probably sneak you both in, if you just stay behind me and sort of keep low – and maybe … don't <u>speak</u> … or squeak."

Ethan grinned. "I'm ready. Going into

incognito mode." And he
pulled his coat up over his head,
looking more suspicious than he did before.

At the front desk there was a tiny grey man

with a drip at the end of his nose. As
Eugenie approached him, he seemed
to puff himself out a little. "Eugenie,
how lovely to see you. How are you?"

Hello, Mr Kank. I'm very well," she
replied sweetly.

"The Archive Room, is it?"

"Oh, yes please. Could I borrow the
electronic pass?"

Ethan and I crouched low behind the desk.

A toddler in a buggy stared at us suspiciously.

But before the kid could make a racket, Eugenie

was handed the pass and we shuffled along

behind her, giving the baby a wave.

Once in the Archive Room, we all relaxed a

bit, pulling off our coats and dumping our bags.

Eugenie beamed at us, obviously excited.

Her eyes searched the bookshelves until she

found the book she'd been talking about.

"Eugenie, have you ever thought about

doing normal stuff … like going to the park?"
I asked.

Ethan shot me a look, but Eugenie just ignored me and flipped through the pages.

"There was this bit about two brothers who used to shapeshift," Eugenie muttered, as she flipped through the book.

We looked at her blankly.

"Shapeshift. You know, when humans transform into other things," she said, as if she was explaining the two-times table.

"Like werewolves? And vampires?" Ethan grinned.

"But Fergus didn't just **turn** into a guinea pig. I <u>wished</u> him into one," I moaned.

'Here it is!" Eugenie exclaimed, laying the book open. I jumped back in horror.

"It's <u>him</u>!" I shrieked, my heart pounding in my chest. "That **weird magician**! I've seen him before! He was … he was … " I scrambled through my memories. Why did I recognise that face? "It's that man on the magic set my Aunt Tink gave me for my birthday!" I stammered. I pulled Fergus out of my pocket and plonked him on the desk.

Ethan visibly froze. "Is that really you, Fergus?" he asked, his voice shaking. He crouched down so he was face-to-face with Fergus' small, soft body. Fergus nodded.

"Fergus, look, it's the spooky man from Aunt Tink's magic set!" I said, and Fergus trotted over to the open book and almost stood on the magician's nose.

"Well, there's got to be some sort of

connection!" Eugenie said, sparkling with energy. "This is too much of a coincidence." She began scanning the text.

"His name was Rollo the Impossible … a flamboyant sorcerer, it says here. His brother Andreas was also a magician. They always performed together and were known for dangerous and daring acts of wizardry. But Rollo was extremely jealous of Andreas, and his desire for the limelight eventually ruined both their careers. In one terrible performance, their last ever together, something went magnificently wrong … "

149

Eugenie stopped reading suddenly, snapped the book shut and shoved it hastily back onto the shelf. I'm sure her face had turned a <u>ghostly</u> <u>white.</u>

"What happened?" I asked, and Fergus squeaked, but Eugenie just stood there with a strange look on her face.

"I think the answer to our problem must lie in your magic set. I don't think this book will help. Come on, let's go and have a look at it," she said, abruptly.

Ethan was still staring at Fergus. He put his

finger near Fergus' nose and Fergus slowly shifted forward to sniff it.

"I don't really know ... what to say ... Fergus. I hope you're OK?"

Fergus nodded, began to purr a little, and crept onto Ethan's outstretched hand.

"Do you want to travel in my pocket?" Ethan asked him.

A wave of jealousy flooded over me. I don't really know who I felt more envious of exactly, and I knew it was ridiculous, but I heard myself saying, a bit too loudly, "Fergus likes to travel with me."

But Fergus twitched his nose and climbed up Ethan's sleeve and inside his coat pocket.

I felt angry. I know I didn't really have a right to. I'm just like Rollo the magician, I thought. Why was I always so resentful of my brother? He was smaller than my pencil case now, but he still made me see red.

"Come on," Eugenie urged. "Let's go."

I'm such an idiot, I thought. I just need to get Fergus back to normal. After that, cross my heart, I would never be mean to him again.

Chapter 17

We dodged Mr Bertolini's restaurant and his guinea-pig stew (I mean, *really?!*) and raced onto my road. We were completely puffed out. All this running around, rescuing guinea pigs and discovering evil magicians was hard work.

We just needed to look at that magic set. The solution had to be in there. It just had to be.

"It's just up here, on the left," I said to Eugenie, slowing down as we came to my block of flats.

Then the world went dark. A massive shadow towered over us. It was Axel Buck.

"You didn't think I'd forgotten about your birthday beats, did you?" he grinned, baring his yellow teeth.

"Get lost, Axel," Eugenie said, her voice trembling a little. I stared at her, impressed. But Axel ignored her and started to march towards me. This was it. I was going to get beaten into a pulp.

Suddenly Fergus flew out of Ethan's coat and launched himself at Axel's face.

Axel leapt backwards. "Aggghhh! <u>Help,</u> help!" he cried. "I hate rodents!"

I couldn't believe it! Then he started waving his arms around like a two-year-old needing a wee. Fergus leapt onto Axel's shoulder and scuttled down the back of his jumper.

"<u>Get this thing off me!</u>" Axel shrieked. He started hopping about and wriggling in all directions. We all stood in stunned silence, watching him whimpering like a baby.

Eventually, Fergus shot out of Axel's trouser leg and back to my feet. I bent down to pick him

155

up as Axel turned and ran up the street, shouting "Mummy!"

"You did it, Fergus! I can't believe it!" I grinned, holding him close.

I couldn't believe that Axel had fled … from us! <u>Result</u>! Fergus had been incredible. I don't know if *I* would have scuttled down Axel Buck's trouser leg. But Fergus had done it – for me. For me!

"Come on," said Eugenie, and we charged, with fresh enthusiasm, into my flat.

Chapter 18

"<u>Disaster!</u>" Aunt Tink screeched in our faces as I unlocked the door. I shoved Fergus back into my pocket.

Aunt Tink was wearing a pineapple print jumpsuit with silver platform shoes. She looked as if she was wearing it all for a bet. She'd also changed her hair colour since this morning, and

now looked as if a pink candy floss
machine had exploded on top of her head.
She was hopping from one platform
shoe to the other. "Emergency! It's an
emergency!" she was screaming.

How could she have found out? "I didn't
know my wish would come true, Aunt Tink,"
I started explaining. "I really didn't want this to
happen to Fergus ... "

"What are you talking about?" Aunt Tink
shrieked. "What's happened to Fergus?"

"*Errr* nothing ... " said Ethan quickly. "So
what's the problem?"

"It's Ruby. She's stuck in the bathroom. The shower is running and I can't get her out!"

We all ran to the bathroom door and I banged my fist against it loudly.

"Ruby, can you hear me? Are you OK in there?"

Silence.

"Please say something, Ruby!" I hammered on the door again.

More silence.

"I'm going to have to break the door down," Aunt Tink stammered.

"You can't," Ethan exclaimed. "That

bathroom is tiny. The door will smash into her."

Lots of silence.

"RUBY!" I bellowed, feeling hot and anxious. "How did you let this happen, Aunt Tink?" I shouted.

"She was covered in paint and I was just trying to clean her up. She must have locked the door when I was searching for a towel!" Great big tears rolled down Aunt Tink's face and dropped off the end of her chin.

I sighed. "Ruby," I said, trying to control the frustration in my voice, "It's my birthday. Can

you sing 'Happy Birthday' to me? Just so we
know you're OK in there?"

A long silence, then a tiny voice trickled out
of the bathroom, like a message from a distant
planet.

"Happy Birthday to Poo," it said.

We all looked at each other with relief.
Ethan sniggered. It didn't matter that Fergus
had taught her the poo version. She was alive.
Now we just had to get her out.

"We should call an emergency locksmith,"
Eugenie suggested, sensibly. Aunt Tink turned to
look at her. "I'm Daniel and Ethan's friend,

Eugenie," she explained, introducing herself. I suppose she *was* our friend now.

"Right, Ruby, you keep singing to Daniel. I'll search on my phone for a locksmith," Aunt Tink agreed, going into the kitchen with Eugenie.

Fergus squeaked in my pocket, but I ignored him. He <u>squeaked</u> again. "Yes, Fergus. I know Ruby is singing, 'Happy Birthday to Poo.' Ha-ha-ha." I pulled him out of my pocket, but he shook his head and squeaked more loudly.

"I think he has an idea," Ethan suggested.

Fergus wriggled free, dropping heavily onto the floor. He lowered his head and stretched

himself out flat, so he could squeeze through the tiny gap at the bottom of the door frame and into the bathroom.

"Furry Fergie!" Ruby shouted gleefully. There was a squeak and the sound of a stool being dragged across the bathroom floor. Then the door swung open, with Fergus hanging onto the doorknob by his teeth. He'd unlocked it! We all looked into the bathroom.

Water was overflowing from the shower. and swilling out into the hall. Ruby, Mr Bumbum and the bathroom were covered in blood-red splats. It looked like a horror movie!

Chapter 19

"Ruby! Are you hurt?" I asked, pulling her close, as Fergus leapt onto her shoulder, sniffing at the messy blobs of red. We both looked at each other anxiously, concerned for our baby sister.

Normally, Fergus and I don't see eye-to-eye over matters involving Ruby. We're always fighting to get her on our side. We argued quite a lot before she came along, but things got serious once we had a little helper who could pinch on command and not get in trouble.

Mum never tells Ruby off for throwing stuff or biting. "She's only a baby!" is her automatic response to any Ruby-related crime, meaning Ruby gets away with everything.

"Ruby's out, Aunt Tink!" Ethan called out. Aunt Tink and Eugenie ran back to the bathroom, just as Fergus quickly slipped back into the safe hiding place of my pocket.

"Thank goodness!" Aunt Tink cried, clearly relieved.

"But she's covered in blood!" I said, horrified. (I wasn't going to let Aunt Tink get off that easily.) "And so is the bathroom."

"Oh, that's just my hair dye ... and paint from the playgroup," Aunt Tink explained, checking Ruby over.

"How did you get her out?" she asked, pulling Ruby into a bear hug.

"Furry Fergie saved me!" Ruby wheezed into Aunt Tink's armpit.

"Fergie? How did Fergie save you?" Aunt Tink said, puzzled.

"She means Urgie ... her,

um, imaginary friend. It's an enormous pink elephant," I said, astonished at my inventiveness. "Ruby must have worked out how to undo the lock!" I was getting good at this, I thought, looking at my friends for confirmation.

"Well done Urgie, always saving the day!" Ethan said.

Well done Urgie!

"Where is Fergie – I mean Fergus – anyway?" Aunt Tink said, peering around. "Oh goodness, was I supposed to pick him up? This is horrendous. I hate being in charge of children."

"No, it's fine, Aunt Tink," I stammered.

"Fergus is still at school. He has extra violin lessons."

"More lessons? Oh! But what were you saying before, about a wish … ?" Aunt Tink looked more confused than usual.

"Oh, just that I wish Fergus hadn't joined the school orchestra. He never has any time off now." I tried really hard to look innocent.

"Oh, well, that's great!" she smiled. "I'm glad you two seem to be getting on better. Last time I saw you guys, you practically tried to kill him with a banana."

Eugenie did that rolling

eyeballs thing at me, like I was the worst brother in the world. I suppose I was.

"We're as close as anything now," I said, feeling Fergus' tiny heartbeat inside my pocket. "Thick as thieves. We almost live in each other's pockets."

"Right, well, now that disaster is over, are you going to open your last present, birthday boy? I think there was another gift left for you in the living room."

"I really want to look at your present properly, Aunt Tink."

I needed to get to that magic set. I was

counting on it holding some
clue to undoing this <u>stupid</u> wish.

"Where did you find it, Aunt Tink?" Ethan
asked. "Daniel told us all about it. It sounds
really cool."

"This amazing junk shop, right on the very
end of the pier where I live. Actually, when
I went to look for it again, the shop had just
disappeared – vanished into thin air, as if it
had never been there. Very odd!"

"Now, open your last present!" she cried
excitedly. There was not much we could do when
Aunt Tink had made her mind up.

Chapter 20

I read the tag attached to the gift. In messy, wonky writing it said:

You're the BEST brother ever. I Saved up all YeaR to get You THis. i hopE You Like it. Love Fergus X

I tore off the crumpled wrapping paper. Inside was a desktop ping-pong table set.

I swallowed. My brother, I realised, had bought me a present, a <u>really</u> <u>great</u> <u>present</u>, with his own money.

He'd been so mean and stingy all year. It had been totally annoying. I had started to call him Scrimper. Any time we were given pocket money, he'd stash his somewhere. (I never found out where and, yes, I'd looked everywhere.) He wouldn't ever lend me any of it – even when I'd run out of change on the 2p machine in the arcade and was just about to win a Black Wasp

key-ring. Or when I wanted to buy extra football stickers and I knew (for certain) that the next packet would have that super-rare hologram one.

Now I understood. All that time, he'd been saving up to buy me a present for my birthday. And I'd given him such a hard time about it.

I felt <u>terrible</u>. What good was a ping-pong table without a life-size brother to play it with?

"Come on Daniel, show us your magic set now!" That was Eugenie, reminding me there was a glimmer of hope that I hadn't ruined

173

my actually quite (dare I say it?) nice brother's life.

"Do your parents know where you are?"
Aunt Tink asked Ethan and Eugenie. "I don't
want any more problems today."

"I should probably call mine," Ethan said,
and Eugenie agreed she'd better let her dad
know where she was, too. They followed Aunt
Tink to the kitchen to borrow her phone.

I headed to my bedroom and shut the door.
I pulled Fergus out of my pocket and sat him on
my desk, looking at him right in his beady
little eyes.

174

I couldn't keep pretending I hated him any more. I didn't. And I think at that moment, the battle between us was over.

Then, in a typical Fergus kind of way, he picked up my rubber and sharpener and began effortlessly juggling them.

I had to admit, it did look quite funny. Even though my brother was now a guinea pig, he couldn't help it, he was just so himself.

And maybe that wasn't so bad?

"You're one of a kind, Fergus,"
I whispered. Then, taking a deep
breath, I said the words I swore
I would **never** say to my brother
under any circumstances.

"I'm sorry."

He looked at me, stunned.

"I'm sorry I turned you into a guinea
pig, Fergus. I'm really sorry I'm always
so mean to you. It's just that it's hard sometimes,
you know, being the oldest. And you're so good
at everything. And I'm not." I sighed. I wasn't
even any good at this. "Thank you for my present.

I am going to get you back to normal. I miss you
… being human, I mean. Although you're quite
good at being a guinea pig, and actually it's been
pretty useful today … "

He shot me a 'Seriously, dude?' kind of look.

"No, of course not. We're going get you back
to being a boy."

Ethan and Eugenie barged into my room. "So
where's the magic set?" Eugenie asked, closing the
door behind her. I pulled it out from under my bed.

"Yikes!" Ethan gasped in horror. The face
on the lid had something really sinister about
it. I tipped off the lid with the back of my hand,

177

worried that something might leap out at us. It didn't. Eugenie tipped the contents out over my bed and Fergus sniffed around the objects: a red ball, a velvet bag, a little hammer and a collapsible top hat. It was just a heap of toys.

"Is that it?" I said, dismayed. "It's just a <u>useless</u> magic kit for kids. How can this help?"

"What about this?" Ethan asked. A little booklet lay at the bottom of the box, faded and crumpled. He handed it automatically to Eugenie.

"Are you all right in there? No one locked in

I hope, ha ha!" Aunt Tink's muffled voice could be heard through the walls.

"Don't come in!" I screeched, looking at Fergus. "We're practicing a magic show for you, Aunt Tink … be out in ten minutes."

"Oh <u>fab!</u>" she said. "Ruby and I will make a stage for you in the living room, and we'll get an audience together!" We heard Aunt Tink start dragging the furniture about.

"I hope she doesn't find that hole we made in the wall last year," Ethan said, nervously.

"If that's all I get in trouble about, then that's fine with me," I replied.

"Mmm, here's a trick to make something disappear." Eugenie murmured, flipping through the pages of the booklet.

"Tricks! I don't need tricks. I need magic. *Real* magic," I said, exasperated. "I thought this guy, Rollo, was an actual wizard or something. What did you say about him earlier? Dark magic, with his brother, on stage?"

Eugenie looked nervous, "I don't know if it will help … knowing *that* much more about Rollo and Andreas."

"Tell us," Ethan and I both insisted, and Fergus gave an affirmative squeak.

Chapter 21

"Well," began Eugenie uncomfortably, "the book in the library said that the two brothers started messing with real magic in their show. And it got out of hand."

"Here we go!" I said brightly.

"One night, Rollo turned his brother, Andreas, into a rabbit on stage,"

she continued. "The audience went wild. No one in the magic community could work out how he'd done it. And Andreas was **never** seen or heard from again. Rollo kept on performing alone, but people lost interest in him without his brother. It was like salt without pepper."

"Rain without an umbrella! A shoe without a sock," Ethan chipped in.

"Yes, thanks, Ethan," I said.

"Like cheese without jam."

"No, not like cheese without jam! That's disgusting, what's wrong with you?" squealed Eugenie.

"Have you tried it?" Ethan countered.

"Go on, Eugenie," I said.

"Well, eventually Rollo disappeared too. No one ever discovered exactly what happened to the brothers, but when their house was finally broken in to … " Eugenie paused. Fergus snorted dramatically.

"Tell us," I urged.

"*Um* … there were rabbit droppings everywhere. And all they found were two dead rabbits, lying in each other's arms, under Rollo's bed."

"Yuck!" Ethan shuddered.

"How is that any help?"

I cried. "Basically you're saying Fergus is stuck like this. And I'm going to turn into a guinea pig too!"

Eugenie kept flipping through the booklet. It was like she didn't want to look me in the eye. This was it, I thought. We're doomed. Fergus is going to be a guinea pig <u>forever</u>.

I looked over at my brother. "This is a nightmare," I screamed, kicking the lid of the empty magic box onto the floor. A piece of paper fluttered out of the squashed cardboard.

"What's this?" I murmured, as I picked it up. "It's a handwritten letter!" I started to read it aloud.

184

Dear Andreas, my one and only brother,

I desperately hope, while reading this, you have transformed into a human once again. How could I have known that wish would work? I am so very sorry for what I did to you and I have tried every spell we were ever taught to try and undo the curse. Life is lonely without you. I was wrong for always wanting the spotlight.

Tonight, I will try the Reverse Morphology spell. I know it's dangerous and I may not survive. But, I hope, instead, we can burn this letter together once we are reunited in human form. If the spell backfires and instead I am transformed into a rabbit, then please follow this spell to release me from the magic and allow me to be human once again:

INGREDIENTS

Mint   *Rose water*

Blessed rice   *Pure basil*

Moroccan oil   Rabbit hair

A human tooth

A treasured item of the transformed human.

Mix and bind the elements in Something
Truthful. Repeat the following incantation, calling the
power of the Universe, at the stroke of midnight, until
the Something Truthful is fully charged:

> **The Moon has awoken, let the Sun sleep on,**
> **We must undo what once was done.**
> **Head to toe, body and mind,**
> **May you, dear brother, return to human kind.**

I know, Andreas, this spell may not keep you
constantly as a human, and there may be temporary
periods of shapeshifting, but this might just work
enough, brother, for our lives to go on – and be better
than ever before!

I cannot wait to hold you in my arms once more,

Rollo X

We all looked at each other. "That's it! We've **got** to try the magic spell!" I exclaimed. "We can find most of these ingredients in the kitchen. *Come on!*"

"What are you talking about?" cried Ethan. "Andreas **didn't** turn back into a human. And Rollo turned into a **rabbit**. They both ended up as rabbits! **Dead** rabbits."

"Yeah. I think we should try something else," Eugenie said nervously. Fergus squeaked in agreement.

"What else *can* we try?" I cried.

There was a loud tap on the door.

"Are you lovely ones ready for your performance?" Aunt Tink called. "And also, when *will* Fergus be home? I'm sure he'd like to see the magic show ... Well, knowing him, he'll probably want to star in it too!"

Chapter 22

"*Um* … we just need to get a few bits for the show," I said, shoving past Aunt Tink and rushing into the kitchen.

There wasn't any Moroccan oil. Surely sunflower oil was sort of the same thing. Dad had a secret stash of mints, so I took one of those (well two actually: I popped one in my

mouth for energy). Now, pure
basil … what was that? A spice?
I found a jar at the back of
the cupboard. The label had
mostly peeled off, but it looked like it might have
once said Basil. It was green, anyway.

"Rice … rice … " I said aloud, flinging open
cupboards.

"Why do you need rice?" Aunt Tink asked
slowly, coming into the kitchen.

"For the show. You'll see," I said, spilling
rice all over the floor. "I'll clear that up later,"
I said, trying to keep my voice steady.

190

"Daniel, when *will* we see Fergus exactly?"

I looked at the pile of ingredients balanced in my arms. "Soon, very soon," I said optimistically, bustling past her.

I didn't have any rose water, but Mum had some posh rose shampoo that she didn't let anyone else use. I grabbed the bottle from the bathroom. I could come up with an excuse for why it was half-empty later.

Now I just needed a *Treasured item* that belonged to Fergus. What did he love more than anything else? I sheepishly remembered his PD

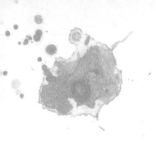

Smith Galaxia Ball. Three weeks ago I'd hidden it in the bathroom because he kept winding me up, calling me Dan the Man. I was a **terrible** person.

"What's going on?" Aunt Tink said, following me as I stuffed my hand down the back of the toilet. "You seem … a bit *agitated*."

"I'm just **excited**," I said.

"Well, I'm really glad you like the magic set this much!" Aunt Tink replied. "But I think Ruby's getting **bored** waiting. I distracted her with some colouring pencils and she drew this. Isn't it **funny**!"

I glanced at it briefly. "Great!" I said.

"But look at Fergus!" she laughed. I studied
it more closely now. Ruby had drawn our family.
There was me, with green hair, and Mum,
Dad and Ruby with matching zombie-style
eyes. Fergus was just a small, brown blob. It
made me feel slightly sick.

Suddenly I had a flash of **inspiration**. "Can I have this?" I asked. Maybe this could be the *Something Truthful* from Rollo's list.

I just needed to get hold of **rabbit hair**. Or was that if you had turned someone into a rabbit? Maybe I needed guinea-pig hair. I found some **scissors** in the kitchen and went back into my room.

"Sorry Fergus, but I'm doing this for you," I said, holding the scissors. Fergus was sitting on my desk, squeaking.

"Daniel, **stop!**" Ethan said,

194

grabbing Fergus. "You're acting **insane**. Just cool it for a second! Let's talk this through. What if **you** turn into a guinea pig, too? You'd be rubbish in goal, for a start … "

"I am going to do this,' I said. "If you come up with a <u>better plan</u>, let me know." I dumped the spell ingredients on my bed.

"Well, there's nowhere you can get a human tooth from is there? So it's all **pointless**," Ethan said negatively.

"I've already thought of that … " I said, taking a piece of string out of my bedside drawer.

"You've got a **wild glint** in your eye, Daniel.

You look like Rollo. Stop and think about what you're doing," Eugenie begged. "What will your parents say when they get back and find out you're both guinea pigs?"

"If you two don't help me, then I'll pull my tooth out myself," I said bluntly. I tied one end of the string around my last milk tooth and the other end to the door handle.

"Are you absolutely sure about this?" Ethan asked. "I don't know if it's ... "

But just then Aunt Tink yanked open the door and my tooth was **ripped** from my gums.

"AGGGHHHHHH!" I yelled in agony.

"What's happened?" she said, stepping into my room, just as Eugenie quickly threw the top hat on top of Fergus. "What did I do?"

Blood was running down my chin, but at least the tooth was out. I grinned, holding it up theatrically.

"My last baby tooth just came out,"
I announced.

"Oh, I'm not that good with blood," Aunt
Tink said, dismayed.

Then the doorbell
suddenly <u>buzzed</u> loudly.
We all looked at each other.

"Who could that be?"
I said.

"That'll be Fergus, at last!" Aunt Tink said,
smiling and sounding relieved. "Just in time for
the show!"

Chapter 23

"Oh, thank you ... Shall I take my shoes off?"
We heard a deep voice trail from the hall.

Eugenie peeped warily into the hallway.
"It's **my dad!** I can see his shoes,"
she hissed. "Look guys, he shouldn't
be here, you're not going to
like him ... He ... "

But before she could explain, Aunt Tink ran back down the hall.

"Come on, you must be ready to start the show by now!" she cried. "It wasn't Fergus at the door, but I guess he'll be back soon. Eugenie and Ethan, I rang your parents to invite them along to see your performance!"

We all looked at each other in disbelief and followed her nervously down the hall. Aunt Tink had transformed our pokey little living room into a spectacular theatre.

Sitting at the back of the room on a
deckchair I had never even seen before was
a man who looked like a **wrinkly,
dad-version** of Eugenie.

"Wow!" I said, taking it all in.

The doorbell buzzed again.

"Er, Aunt Tink, we weren't really planning a
sell-out performance … " I stuttered.

201

"Nonsense," said Aunt Tink. She opened the door wide and Fatima, Ethan's mum, stood there smiling. Then I heard her call out, "Mr Bertolini!" from the hall balcony. "You must come up! Daniel's about to perform a birthday magic show."

Not Mr Bertolini! I thought.

"I was just taking Snowball for a walk, but anything for you, Tinkerbell! Come on, Snowball." Snowball is the vicious creature Mr Bertolini calls a dog. We could hear Mr Bertolini's footsteps and

202

Snowball's muted growls as they approached the front door.

"Let the show begin!" Aunt Tink announced, as Ethan, Eugenie and I stood huddled in the hallway.

"What are we going to do?" I cried. "We don't know any magic tricks!"

"Don't worry, I've seen loads of magic shows on YouTube. I've got this," Ethan said smoothly. He ran to my bedroom and grabbed some of the props from Rollo's magic set.

"Welcome to the fabulous and mysterious Magic Birthday Show!" he said, walking onto the makeshift stage. "We're **really glad** to have you here! First of all, I need something from the audience ... Aha!"

He leaned forward and whipped Aunt Tink's orange glasses right off her nose.

"Oh, I need those!" she spluttered. But Ethan had already placed them inside the little velvet bag. Before anyone could stop him, he ⁻smashed the bag with the tiny magician's hammer.

"<u>My glasses!</u>" Aunt Tink shrilled. "I *will*

need those back, Ethan. I can't see anything without them."

I dragged Ethan back out into the hallway. "What are you doing?" I hissed.

"That's what they do all the time in magic shows," he said. "Don't worry!"

Ruby came toddling out of my bedroom, wearing the top hat. She was holding Fergus in one hand and Mr Bumbum in the other.

"Fergie!" she cried. "Magic show, Fergie!"

"No, Ruby! Put Fergus back in my bedroom. We need to

perform magic tricks!" Then I had a <u>brainwave</u>. "Actually, can we use Mr Bumbum?" I asked, trying to prize Mr Bumbum out of her hands.

"Noooo," she cried, holding on as if her life depended on it.

"Listen, Ruby, I'll make Mr Bumbum appear out of the hat. Everybody'll love it. Then they can all go home and I can get on with turning Fergus back into a human. You *want* that, don't you?"

Ruby looked doubtful, but reluctantly handed me Mr Bumbum. Fergus clambered up Ethan's leg and hid in his top pocket.

Chapter 24

I rushed out onto the stage. "My trusty assistant, Ruby," I said dramatically, pulling her from the hallway, "is going to make a rabbit appear out of this hat!"

The audience whooped and clapped in anticipation.

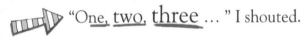 "One, two, three ... " I shouted.

"Abracadabra!" Ethan yelled. He lunged into the room and threw a bottle of pink glitter at the audience.

"Ugh, it's gone in my mouth!" Mr Bertolini yelled. He began **spitting glitter** so violently that his brown toupée came **flying** off his head!

At that exact moment, I pulled Mr Bumbum <u>triumphantly</u> out of the hat, just as Snowball leapt into the air to grab it, gnashing her teeth and knocking Ethan over. As Ethan fell, Fergus **tumbled** out of his pocket and **plopped** onto the floor, right next to Mr Bertolini's stranded hairpiece.

"Oh, Mr Bertolini, your hair!" Aunt Tink squeaked in shock, and, grabbing Fergus, she placed him smoothly onto Mr Bertolini's bald head.

We all stared at Mr Bertolini in horror.

"What's wrong?" Aunt Tink asked. "Don't be embarrassed, Mr Bertolini, I think your toupée looks very nice! Right, I'm going to have to find my back-up glasses until you magic my first pair

back, Ethan. I really can't see a thing." And with that, she swept out of the room.

We stood there on the stage, not sure what to do next, until Snowball began sniffing at Mr Bertolini's head. Realising that Fergus was not actually a wig, she jumped up and tried to grab him.

"Down girl!" Mr Bertolini said, backing away. "Bad dog!"

Fergus fell clumsily off Mr Bertolini's shiny head and landed in Fatima's lap.

"A mouse, it's a mouse!" she screeched,

clambering onto a wobbly kitchen stool. Poor Fergus was catapulted onto the floor, where he was immediately spotted by Snowball.

"This is it. This the end!" I gasped in horror.

"It's OK everybody," Eugenie's dad said calmly, swiftly picking Fergus up. He held him high above Snowball's head.

"Fergus!" I yelped.

"I'm going to take Snowball out," Mr Bertolini said, embarrassed. "Please tell Tink I say good-bye. Happy birthday again, Daniel." He yanked Snowball towards the door

with one hand, the other firmly clamped over his real toupée.

"Did somebody say 'Fergus'?" Aunt Tink flounced back into the room wearing her enormous, glittery prescription sunglasses and seemingly unaware of the chaos surrounding her.

"Um … why is there a guinea pig in the house? Was it part of the magic show?" she asked, looking very confused.

Chapter 25

"I've **never** seen it before in my life!" I said defensively. "I think we must have a guinea pig infestation. They get in and eat all the crumbs … "

"Guinea pigs? Don't you mean **mice**?" Aunt Tink asked, sounding even more confused.

"Please … are there any **mice** in here?" Fatima asked, still trembling on top of the stool.

"Listen everyone, it's fine. I work in a
science laboratory," said Eugenie's dad.
"We use guinea pigs like this one every day for
medical research. I'll drop this little fella into the
lab on my way home and he'll be put to good use."
"What do you mean?" I whispered, aghast.
I felt very weak all of a sudden. I couldn't let
Eugenie's dad take Fergus to a science lab.
I could just imagine them carrying out
medical experiments on him, wiring
him up or injecting him with chemicals.
"I'll find a shoe box for you to put it in."
Aunt Tink searched around till she found the

214

box my new football boots came in. Didn't she hear what Eugenie's dad said? Was she crazy? A SCIENCE LAB!

"Perfect," Eugenie's dad said, carefully placing Fergus into the box. As the lid was closed I looked at Eugenie and Ethan in horror. I had no idea what to do.

Ruby put her little hand in mine and yanked me out into the hallway. "Swap for Fergie," she whispered, holding up Mr Bumbum (who was now covered in glitter).

I glanced through the doorway

at the box on Eugenie's dad's lap. "OK, Rubes, good idea," I agreed.

"Where are your shoes, Eugenie?" her dad asked. Eugenie gave me a meaningful glance and dragged her dad around the flat, saying, "Oh, I don't know where I left them! Silly me!"

Ruby and I crept up to the box and swiftly grabbed Fergus, who was trembling with fear. "It's OK, I've got you," I said, and tucked him into my pocket.

Ruby gave Mr Bumbum a final squeeze, then put him in the box. We managed to close the lid just as Eugenie's dad walked back into the room.

Chapter 26

I waved good-bye to my friends
at the door. Eugenie's dad was
holding the shoe box under his arm.

"What's your dad going to say when he gets
to the lab and there's just a soft toy in there?"

Ethan hissed at Eugenie.

"I don't know!" she giggled,

"but I'll make sure I get **Mr Bumbum** back to Ruby."

"Are you going to be OK, Daniel? What are you going to do about the spell?" Eugenie asked, her eyes round and worry on her face.

"<u>Please</u> don't try it, Daniel," Ethan insisted. "We'll think of something else to try tomorrow."

"It's OK. Fergus and I have got this," I whispered back to my friends. I didn't want to think about what would happen if the spell backfired or, worse, if it didn't work at all.

"I can't believe Fergus missed all that

excitement!" Aunt Tink said. "He would have loved the magic show! He can't still be in violin lessons, can he?"

What was I meant to say now? Rollo had said that the spell had to be performed at midnight.

"I just remembered," Eugenie said confidently. "It's the 'Orchestra Sleep-over at School' event tonight."

"That's right, I forgot to tell you, Aunt Tink, Fergus is staying at school tonight. He's been really excited about it for weeks."

Aunt Tink looked concerned. "Did he take his pyjamas? Was he meant to have a packed

lunch – I mean supper? I don't remember your parents telling me anything about a school sleep-over."

I took a breath and replied with conviction. "Yes. He has a tuna and sweetcorn sandwich and a chocolate bar. He made it last night. My parents did tell you about it, remember?"

"*Um* … OK then," Aunt Tink said, baffled.

"Well, 'bye Daniel," Ethan said, looking really worried. "I hope we'll see you – and Fergus – at school tomorrow."

"Of course you will," I said through <u>gritted teeth</u>.

He gave me a tight hug.

"Be careful," he whispered into my ear. Then they all left, leaving me standing in the doorway.

"Well, it's a shame Fergus isn't here. As a birthday treat, I thought we could go out for supper to Bertolini's," Aunt Tink said, smiling. "Your mum told me they're always trying out new dishes from around the world. I think I saw today's. It's … "

I had no desire to see Mr Bertolini or his dog again. "Can we go tomorrow Aunt Tink? When Fergus can come with us."

Aunt Tink looked disappointed, but then

perked up when she remembered a recipe for
banana and mayonnaise hot dogs. (I
couldn't eat anything anyway. Not after
imagining Fergus served on a plate of rice.)
I just needed to get to midnight. I just wanted
to see Fergus' <u>freckly</u> human face again.

I told Aunt Tink I was super-tired after such
a busy day and shut myself (and Fergus) in my
room. I read through Rollo's list once again.
I just had to get the last item. I found the
kitchen scissors and looked at Fergus.

He gave a squeak
(which I took to be a

yes), so I snipped off a tuft of reddy-brown frizz from the top of his head.

I added the tuft to the pile of ingredients I'd heaped onto Ruby's drawing. Then I added a large dollop of Mum's shampoo and mixed it all together. Mashed bits of flaky green basil and rodent hair floated in the oil.

Would this really work? I took a <u>deep breath</u>, stuck my tiny, white tooth deep into the potion and folded up the paper.

There was a timid knock at the door. "Furry Fergie?" a muffled little voice whispered.

Chapter 27

I sighed and let Ruby in. If
everything went wrong, this might
be the <u>last time</u> she would
see me without paws and whiskers.

She dragged her dolls' house across the
carpet and, with a lot of effort, pulled it up onto
Fergus' bed. She picked up Fergus from my desk

and carefully placed
him in the miniature
four-poster, pink plastic bed. At least if this all
went wrong, Fergus and I could live in comfort.

"Night-night, Fergie. Night-night, Daniel,"
she said, and gave us both a kiss on the cheek.

"Good night, Rubes. Will you be OK without
Mr Bumbum tonight?" She nodded solemnly
and scampered off to her own bedroom.

I looked at Fergus in the little house. He
actually looked quite comfy in his plastic bed.
"This had better work," I said.

I checked my watch. It was 11.55 pm. My heart began to beat loudly in my chest and my hands were shaking. I got the potion ready and finally pulled out Rollo's letter from the magic kit, to read the spell aloud. Fergus had climbed out of the doll's bed and was now sitting on top of the little package of rather damp ingredients, wrapped in Ruby's folded drawing.

<u>Three</u> ... <u>Two</u> ... <u>One</u> ... it was exactly
midnight! My voice was croaky as I read Rollo's
fateful words. What had he done wrong that had
made the spell fail so badly? I knew I definitely
did not want to be turned into a guinea pig.
I just wanted everything back to normal.

"The Moon has awoken," I began, "let the
Sun sleep on. We must undo what once was done."
I paused. "Fergus, is this really going to work?"

He nodded, encouragingly.

"OK, OK. Head to toe, body and mind. May
you, dear brother, return to
human-kind."

227

We waited and stared at each other. Fergus' alarm clock ticked noisily, but nothing happened. There was no white light, or weird slow motion. Just a slight sickly smell of flowery shampoo mixed with mints.

It wasn't going to work. That was it. I'd have to tell Aunt Tink. Mum and Dad would find out. Our lives, as we knew it, would be over.

I kept staring at Fergus, willing any part of him to look a bit more human.

Just his feet would do.

In the gloomy light, he seemed to be more <u>rodenty</u> than ever.

After a while he closed his eyes and started making soft little sleepy snorts.

The least I can do is make him comfortable, I thought. I carried him to his plastic dolls' house bed and stroked his tufty head.

Chapter 28

I woke up feeling hot and sticky. "Fergus, get out of my bed," I said automatically, shoving my brother's arm off me.

"Why do you always get into my bed? And where are your pyjamas?" I began. But then I saw the dolls' house and the little parcel of spell ingredients on my table.

"Fergus!" I yelled. "You're a … a … human!" I jumped around the room. YES! "Fergus, it's you! You're really you again!"

He gave me a sleepy smile and I launched towards him, giving him a massive hug. Then I remembered he was naked. Yewk!

I didn't want to be weird about it, but I carefully looked him over, checking that all his bits were human.

He was perfect! No fur anywhere. Only his fringe was missing, just a clump of short hairs sticking up on end.

"Fergus! Say something!" I demanded.

Please, I thought,
don't squeak.

"Shall we play with
the ping-pong set now?"
he said, smiling.

Woo hoo! YES! My bro! The verruca
I can't live without! The scab I can't wait to
itch! He's back! I had this weird mix of
feelings come all over me.

"Darling … darling … I can't get in." Aunt
Tink was calling from behind the door. I'd
wedged the chair against it last night. I pulled it
out of the way and she flew into the room,

New hair!

holding her phone. "It's your parents, they're calling from Scotland. Fergus?" she said, confused. "I thought you were at school on a sleep-over. Where are your pyjamas?"

"*Um* … he arrived home early this morning, and he's just going to have a shower," I mumbled, snatching the phone.

"Mum, Dad?" I said, nervously.

It was Mum. "Daniel, we are <u>so, so sorry</u>."

"Sorry for what?" I asked, exchanging a glance with my brother.

"We tried absolutely everywhere to get reception on our phones. It's just impossible in the Scottish Highlands. We took a taxi to the local town this morning and at last we've got through to you. We wanted to wish you a happy birthday for yesterday, of course. Did you have a lovely day?" Mum asked.

"*Um*, it was memorable," I said.

"Well, that's good. Aunt Tink told us about your magic show. It sounded, um, *eventful*. And I hope you've not been giving your brother

234

too much of a hard time, Daniel. You know he's only seven and he does love you."

I looked at my over-the-top, loud, obnoxious little brother. "I love him too, Mum."

There was a stunned silence on the other end of the phone. Fergus threw himself at me in a bear hug and wrapped his arms tightly around my waist.

"Oh, great, wow, that's so lovely to hear," Mum said at last. "Here's Dad."

"Hi Dan, happy birthday!

Listen, before we lose reception again, I wanted to explain about the plant."

My hand gripped the phone more tightly.

"We know you really want a pet, but we couldn't leave you a pet while we were away. Aunt Tink had enough on her plate keeping tabs on you three, without a furry little creature in the flat as well. So we want you to know that, when we get home tomorrow, we are all going to the pet shop, and we've already reserved you ... a guinea pig!"

I was silent.

"A guinea pig, Daniel! Say something!

We thought you'd be over the moon. Can you imagine, your own guinea pig to look after?"

"You know what, Dad," I replied. "I'm really happy with the plant."